Sollie was a timid puppy.
He did not like to go
down the stairs.

His owner had to carry
him down the stairs to
take him out for a walk.

Sollie saw a horse when
he was on the walk, and
his eyes opened wide.
He jumped into the lap
of his owner.

Sollie went to the park.
He watched the shelties
run. They ran fast and
looked grand.

Sollie wished to run with
the shelties in the fields
of lilies and daisies.

"I can not wait until I
am a brave terrier like
my dad," Sollie said
to himself.

6

By the summer, Sollie had grown up a lot. He went to the beach with his owner and ran up and down the pier.

When Sollie ran down
to the beach, a toddler
held out her hand with
some cookie pieces.
Sollie ate them.

Sollie watched the toddler and her mom walk down to the water to dip their feet in the cool waves.

The waves were wet and cold. The toddler shrieked, "Wa-a-a-a!" Then her pail fell into the water.

The waves took the pail out far. The toddler's mom did not reach it.

Sollie knew just what
to do. With strong,
graceful leaps, he ran
into the waves.

Sollie swam with strong
strokes. He got the
handle of the pail
in his teeth.

Sollie swam back
to shore and ran
to the toddler.
He let the pail drop
at the toddler's feet.

The toddler gave Sollie
a hug and said,
"Good doggie."
The toddler's mom said,
"You are such a brave dog!
I believe you are a hero!"

Sollie felt such pride.
Sollie felt strong.
Sollie knew that he was
now a brave terrier.